NEVER SAY
DIE

PAIRED:

Two men who had to fight for their lives. Aron Ralston
(left), a solo adventurer, was trapped in a desert
wilderness. Joe Simpson, a mountain climber,
was left for dead at 17,000 feet.

"We've all got a reason to keep living. It may not be pretty, but surviving is grit and determination in its highest form."

Aron Ralston

"I went beyond caring whether I lived or died so long as I did not have to die alone. I wanted a hand to hold, a voice to hear. I craved for some human contact that might alleviate the terrifying emptiness of those days spent slowly dying."

Joe Simpson

Photographs © 2011: Alamy Images: 17 (Extreme Sports Photo), 31 (Thomas Frey/imagebroker), 66 (Martin Harvey), 22, 37, 43 (Beth Wald/Aurora Photos); AP Images/E. Pablo Kosmicki: 52; Aurora Photos: 87 (Mario Colonel), 83 (Jerry Dodrill), 77 (Richard Durnan), 63 (Marcos Ferro), 64 (Ben Moon), 20 (Corey Rich); Brian Hall: back cover right, 3 right, 58, 94, 100; Getty Images/ Gordon Wiltsie: cover; Howie Silleck: 81 (Benjamin Milla), 61, 69, 74; Jan Bryndal: 54; Kobal Collection/Picture Desk: 90 (Film Four/Pathe), 84 (Jeremy Sutton-Hibbert/Film Four/Pathe); Courtesy of Leatherman Tool Group, Inc.: 27; Polaris Images: 48 (Daniel Bayer), back cover left, 3 left (Aron Ralston); Redux Pictures/Kevin Moloney/The New York Times: 14; ShutterStock, Inc./Studio 1One: 44; Superstock, Inc./Glow Images: 28; Courtesy of Ute Mountaineer: 38.

Illustrations by CCI: 54; XNR Productions: 10, 51.

Library of Congress Cataloging-in-Publication Data

McCollum, Sean.
Never say die / Sean McCollum.
p. cm. — (On the record)
Includes bibliographical references and index.
ISBN-13: 978-0-531-22524-0 (alk. paper)
ISBN-10: 0-531-22524-0 (alk. paper)
1. Mountaineering accidents—Juvenile literature. 2.
Mountaineers—Juvenile literature. I. Title.
GV200.M395 2011
796.52'2--dc22

                                    2010040759

Tod Olson, Series Editor
Marie O'Neill, Creative Director
Curriculum Concepts International, Production

Copyright © 2012 Scholastic Inc.

2 3 4 5 6 7 8 9 10   40   21 20 19 18 17 16 15 14 13 12

 Pages printed on 10% PCW recycled paper

NEVER SAY DIE

Would they have what it takes to make it out alive?

DIE

Sean McCollum

Contents

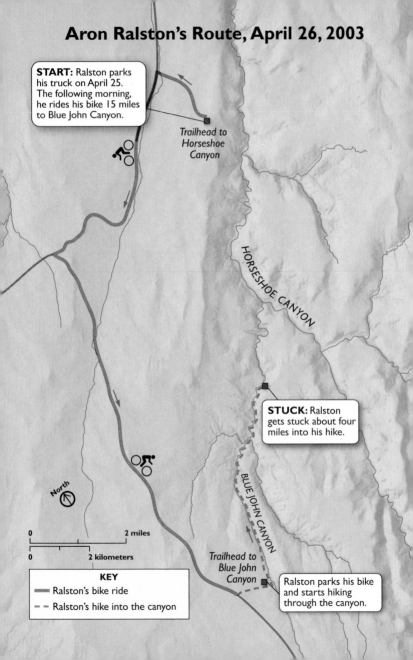

Aron Ralston's Route, April 26, 2003

START: Ralston parks his truck on April 25. The following morning, he rides his bike 15 miles to Blue John Canyon.

Trailhead to Horseshoe Canyon

HORSESHOE CANYON

STUCK: Ralston gets stuck about four miles into his hike.

BLUE JOHN CANYON

Trailhead to Blue John Canyon

Ralston parks his bike and starts hiking through the canyon.

North

0	2 miles

0	2 kilometers

KEY
— Ralston's bike ride
- - - Ralston's hike into the canyon

ESCAPE FROM BLUE JOHN CANYON

In April 2003, Aron Ralston set out for a day trip in the Utah desert. A freak accident turned a lonely canyon into a prison. Ralston had to face the unthinkable to get out alive.

1
Into the Desert

Aron Ralston was alone in the wilderness, and that's the way he wanted it.

On Saturday morning, April 26, 2003, Ralston woke up in the bed of his pickup truck. He was parked at the trailhead to Utah's rugged Horseshoe Canyon. He was in the middle of a five-day vacation. The scorching heat of the desert summer was still weeks away. It was a good day for a solo adventure.

Aron Ralston was photographed in Boulder, Colorado, in 2009. By the time he visited Blue John Canyon, Ralston had climbed 45 of Colorado's 14,000-foot peaks alone and in the winter.

To get to this remote spot, Ralston had driven 240 miles from his home in Aspen, Colorado. A year earlier he had quit his job as an engineer to work in a gear shop for climbers, hikers, and skiers. His new job gave him time to do the things he loved, and he was taking advantage of it. On Thursday he had climbed Mount Sopris in Colorado. Friday he went mountain biking in Moab, Utah.

Today he had a more elaborate plan. He would ride his mountain bike 15 miles to the entrance into Blue John Canyon. From there he would scramble back to his truck through Blue John and Horseshoe canyons. It was an ambitious plan for an ordinary tourist. But Ralston was neither ordinary nor a tourist.

At 27, the tall, lanky redhead had years of experience in the wilderness. His family had moved to Colorado when he was 12. He grew up skiing, backpacking, and rock climbing.

By the time he left college, he was hooked on adventure. In 1997, Ralston started scaling Colorado's 14,000-foot peaks. He decided he would climb all 59 of the state's "fourteeners"—in the winter and by himself. No one had ever accomplished that feat, and by the spring of 2003, Ralston was more than halfway there.

With that kind of experience behind him, the Utah trip seemed easy. He had planned it at the last minute. He hadn't told anyone where he was going. But he wasn't worried. He would make it back to Aspen by Tuesday with no problem.

In Blue John Canyon, the gap between the walls can
be as narrow as 18 inches. Experienced climbers often
use a technique called "bridging" (above) to move
through tight spaces.

Ralston arrived at Blue John Canyon at about 10:30 on Saturday morning. He locked his bike to a tree. Then he shouldered his 25-pound backpack and headed into the canyon.

Blue John is a slot canyon cut into rocky red sandstone. Slot canyons are deep and narrow. They resemble twisted hallways that open to the sky. Skilled hikers like Ralston think of them as obstacle courses.

Ralston hiked northeast between the canyon walls, navigating the obstacles. The canyon narrowed in places, and he turned sideways to squeeze through. Sometimes the floor dropped off sharply as the canyon carved deeper into the earth. Ralston had to climb down, searching carefully for handholds and footholds in the rock.

Four miles into the hike, he reached a series of giant boulders suspended between the canyon walls. These boulders are known as chockstones. They are carried down the canyon by powerful flash floods until they get stuck in narrow passages.

Ralston crawled under some of the chockstones and climbed over others. At the top of one refrigerator-sized chockstone, he found himself facing a 12-foot drop to the canyon floor. A few feet out and down sat another chockstone the size of a truck tire. Ralston decided to use that smaller boulder as a stepping-stone. He would climb onto it and then drop to the canyon floor.

Ralston gave the smaller chockstone several kicks. It seemed to be wedged tightly enough to hold him. He felt it wobble when he stepped onto it, but that was not

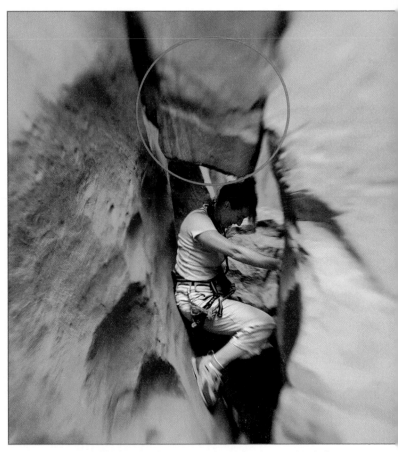

A climber makes her way under a chockstone (circled) in Blue John Canyon. Heavy rainfall can produce flash floods powerful enough to lift boulders and deposit them between the canyon walls.

unusual. He turned around and squatted. He gripped the back of the chockstone. Then he lowered himself so his legs slid over the front of the rock.

Suddenly, the boulder shifted under his weight. He immediately let go and dropped to the ground. He glanced up. The chockstone was rolling right at him. His arms shot up to protect his head.

The chockstone slammed Ralston's left hand against one wall. He jerked that hand away. But the boulder lurched to the other wall and crushed his right hand. It slid another foot and stopped about four feet off the ground.

In a matter of seconds it was over. Ralston could not believe his eyes. His right hand was trapped, smashed between the chockstone and the canyon wall.

Ralston's hand was stuck between the chockstone
on the left and the canyon wall on the right.
(The chockstone was moved after the accident.)

2
Trapped!

A moment passed before the blinding pain shot through Ralston's arm. He swore and tried to yank his hand out. It was hopelessly pinned.

He burst into frantic action. He braced his feet on the canyon floor and leaned into the boulder to try to lift it. He tried again and again, slamming his body into the rock. "Come on … move!" he growled. The chockstone did not budge.

He paused, breathing hard. With his free hand, he unstrapped his backpack and pulled out his water bottle. He took a long drink before he realized his mistake. If he was stuck, he would need to conserve water.

For the first time he stopped to consider his situation. The pain had vanished. He had no feeling in his right hand at all. His wrist had been smashed nearly flat. The chockstone had to weigh at least 800 pounds. And it was wedged solidly between the canyon walls.

A terrible thought hit him like an electric shock. He had made the most basic mistake of solo adventuring: He hadn't told anyone about his plans. No friend or family member knew where he was. And hikers almost never came down Blue John Canyon.

If he was going to escape, he would have to do it himself.

Ralston opened his backpack and examined his supplies. He had two burritos, a CD player, a camcorder, a headlamp, sunglasses, rope, and other climbing gear. One by one he set them on top of the chockstone in front of him. He also had a cheap multi-tool. This all-in-one tool included pliers, a file, and two knife blades.

Ralston's biggest concern was water. He held up the gray plastic bottle. He had 22 ounces left—less than three cups. He would not survive long after the supply ran out.

He examined the boulder that trapped his arm. Maybe he could break off enough rock to free his hand. He began attacking the chockstone with the long knife from his multi-tool.

As the afternoon wore on, he realized he would never be able to chip away enough of the hard rock. But the task kept him busy—and warm. Night fell, and the temperature dropped into the 50s, then the 40s. Ralston wore nothing but shorts, a red T-shirt, a blue baseball cap, wool socks, and running shoes. He clicked on his headlamp and kept working.

For a moment the idea of cutting off his arm occurred to him. He quickly pushed the bizarre thought out of his mind.

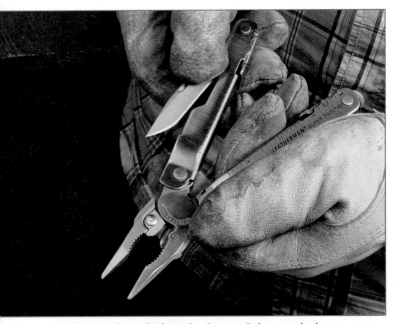

For his trip through Blue John Canyon, Ralston packed
a multi-tool like this one. But his was a cheap version.
It came free with the purchase of a flashlight.

A climber in a black climbing harness ascends a rock wall. The harness keeps her safely attached to the rope even if she loses her grip.

3
Every Way but Loose

In the darkness, Ralston tried desperately to get comfortable. When the boulder pinned his arm, he had been caught in a standing position. He needed to take his weight off his feet.

Ralston decided to build himself a seat. He put on his climbing harness. He slid his feet through the leg loops and strapped the harness around his waist. He scanned the canyon walls above for a place to attach a rope.

He studied the giant chockstone he had tried to descend ten hours earlier. Between the chockstone and the wall of the canyon was a small gap. If only he could get a rope stuck in the gap!

Using his left hand and teeth, he tied a knot at the end of his rope. Then he snapped on a few carabiners—metal clips used for climbing. Ralston was right-handed, but now he had to throw with his left.

After several clumsy tosses, the carabiners dropped into the gap. He jerked the rope, and they wedged tightly. He attached the other end of the rope to his harness. He pulled the rope until his harness supported him in a sitting position. He sighed with relief.

Able to relax for a moment, Ralston calculated his chance of being rescued. It was

Carabiners like this one are used to connect ropes and other gear. The top part is hinged and can be opened to slip ropes and straps on and off.

now early Sunday morning. He wasn't scheduled to work until Tuesday. No one would miss him until he failed to show up. It would be two more days before anyone even *started* to look for him.

By Tuesday he could easily be dead. Dehydration would set in when he ran out of water. He might die of hypothermia as he lost body heat to the cold nights. Heavy rain could send a flash flood down the canyon and drown him.

He returned to chipping at the rock.

Later, he devised another plan to free himself. He looped a rope over and around the giant chockstone above him. He tied a carabiner to the rope. Then he tied another line around the boulder that had trapped him. He ran the line through the carabiner to create a pulley system.

When the system was ready he pulled on the line as hard as he could. The boulder did not budge. He added a loop to the line so he could step on it to add more force. He heaved, swearing, but the rock didn't even tremble.

Sweating and discouraged, Ralston took a break. He was running out of options. The bizarre thought returned to his mind. Could he actually cut off his lower arm?

He checked the knives on the multi-tool. They were dull but they might be able to cut through skin and muscle. He tied a strap around his right arm and tightened it into a tourniquet. If he was lucky, the tourniquet would keep him from bleeding to death. But how would he cut through the two bones in his forearm? The knives were not nearly sharp enough.

Ralston began to face the real possibility that he would die. He took out his camcorder and aimed it at himself. He was sure no one would see the recording until his body was found. But he had things he wanted to say to his family and friends.

He explained what had happened. He pointed the camera at the place where his arm disappeared behind the boulder. Then he added a good-bye message to his parents and to his sister, Sonja.

Ralston shivered through Sunday night and into Monday morning. He hadn't slept in 48 hours.

On Monday afternoon, Ralston took out his camcorder again. He recorded more messages to his friends and family. He thanked them for all their love and for the good times they had enjoyed together. He told them where he wanted his ashes spread after his body was found.

Later, Ralston peed into a container. He looked in disgust at the dark yellow liquid. But at least he would have something to drink after he ran out of water.

Tuesday dawned after another sleepless night. A rescue effort might start soon. But how would they know where to look?

Ralston drank the last of his water. He was running out of time—fast.

Wednesday morning came. He raised the container holding his dark yellow urine. Every so often, he forced himself to choke down a mouthful. He drifted in and out of a daze. He felt like death was only hours away.

Another day ended. Another long, cold

night descended. Earlier, he had scratched his name "ARON" onto the red rock wall beside him. Now he added the month and year he was born: "OCT 75." Below his name, he etched "APR 03" and "RIP"— *Rest in Peace.*

During his ordeal, Ralston scratched the date he expected to die into the canyon wall.

Ralston worked at this store in Aspen, Colorado. He sold outdoor equipment to campers, climbers, skiers, and hikers.

4

Breaking Free

While Ralston inscribed his own tombstone, a rescue effort was underway.

When Ralston did not show up at the store where he worked, his boss became alarmed. Missing a shift was not Ralston's style. The manager called Ralston's roommate and then his mother, Donna Ralston, at the family home in Denver.

Ralston's friends and his mother moved into action. They alerted the police. Then they called or emailed anyone who might have a clue where Aron had gone. Donna Ralston looked through the messages in her son's email account. A friend found an email with a list of Utah canyons that Ralston had said he would like to explore.

Meanwhile, the police accessed Ralston's debit card account. The last purchases had been made in Utah. By 7 A.M. Thursday morning, officials in Utah were checking trailheads for Ralston's pickup truck.

That same morning, as the sun rose over the canyon, Ralston felt like he was reaching the end. He had already lasted two days longer than he had expected. He decided to take a closer look at his trapped hand. He poked at the base of his thumb with the knife. It let out a hiss of gas that smelled like bad meat. His hand had started to rot.

The realization set off a wave of disgust and anger. Ralston screamed and slammed his body against the chockstone again and again. As he thrashed, he felt his right arm bend strangely.

He stopped his outburst. In a flash of insight, he knew exactly what he had to do.

He knelt down and slid his left arm under the boulder. He pushed with all his might, twisting his trapped arm downward. A crack sounded in the canyon. He had snapped one of his arm bones.

He stood up and adjusted his position. He pressed his feet against the rock wall. He reached over the boulder and pulled with his left arm. *SNAP!* The other bone broke.

The sound filled Ralston with excitement. He drew a knife blade on his multi-tool and started the gruesome task he had been considering for days. He sliced through the skin of his forearm and revealed the tissue underneath.

He began slicing through the muscle. Then he paused to tie a tourniquet on his arm. He used the pliers to tear at the tendons, the cord-like tissues that connect muscles to bones. He cut through the arteries.

He had cut most of the way through when he touched the blade to a bundle of nerves. As he cut, a searing pain shot through his upper body. He felt like he was being burned alive.

After nearly an hour, Ralston cut through the last stretch of skin. He pulled away, leaving his wrist and hand trapped against the wall. For the first time in six days, he was free.

He had just amputated his own hand, and yet he felt as though he had been reborn.

The canyon wall to the right was marked with Ralston's blood.

A climber rappels down a steep rock face. Rappelling allows climbers to control the speed at which they slide down a rope.

5
Rescue!

Ralston had freed himself from his prison, but he was a long way from safety. It was an eight-mile hike through the rest of the canyon to his truck. From there he would have to drive miles more to get help. He was exhausted, dehydrated, and losing blood fast.

He wrapped the stump of his arm in plastic to keep it clean. He arranged his backpack to act as a sling. He packed up his gear and moved out.

He stumbled along the canyon floor. After a few hundred feet, the narrow canyon opened and the floor dropped off sharply. Ralston stood at the top of a 65-foot cliff known as the Big Drop.

When he began the hike, Ralston had known about the Big Drop. He had planned to rappel down the cliff—lower himself with a rope. He just hadn't expected to do it with one hand.

Still, there was no other way out. He pulled out his climbing equipment and tied his rope to a bolt that was already anchored in the cliff. Then he fed the line through his harness. A belay plate would allow him to slow his descent by controlling the friction on the rope. For a strong climber with two hands, the descent would not have been difficult. But for Ralston, on the verge of exhaustion, it could have been a death sentence.

Ralston looked down and saw a puddle of water next to the bottom of the drop. That gave him a new burst of courage. He backed off the cliff and trusted his life to his skills. He took it slowly at first, and then sped up as he glided down the line.

When his feet finally hit the ground, he lunged at the puddle. Gladly, he poured out the last of his urine from the water bottle. He filled it and guzzled the first water he had drunk in two days. He drank one bottle-ful, then another.

Stocking up on water, he set out for his truck. The midday sun blazed overhead. His heart hammered in his chest, working hard to make up for the loss of blood. He feared he might pass out if he pushed too hard.

After amputating his arm, Ralston hiked to an opening in the slot canyon (circled). Then he rappelled 65 feet down the Big Drop (marked with a white line).

About two miles from the trailhead, he spotted a party of hikers. At first he thought he was hallucinating. Then he realized they were real. "HELP!" he shouted. "HELP! I NEED HELP!"

In a moment, a family of three stood in front of him—the first people he had seen in six days. The man said simply, "They told us you were here."

With help from the man and another hiker, Ralston stumbled through the last two miles. As he neared the trailhead, a helicopter appeared over the canyon wall. It descended into the canyon and landed on the dry riverbed.

"Can I get a lift?" Ralston asked the pilot before climbing in.

As they lifted off, Ralston felt like crying. But his body was too dehydrated to produce tears.

The story of Ralston's escape made news around the globe. Along with his hand, he had lost 40 pounds and more than three pints of blood. In 2004, he published *Between a Rock and a Hard Place.* The book tells the chilling story of those six days, along with accounts of his other expeditions.

Ralston's experience in Blue John Canyon did not dampen his love of the outdoors. After his accident, he started using a custom-made prosthetic arm for climbing, skiing, and other outdoor sports.

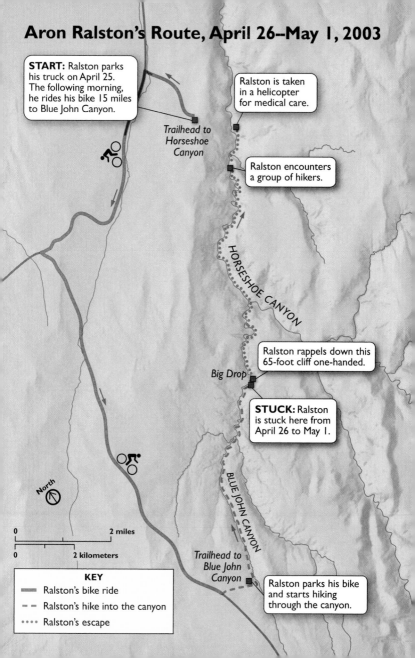

Aron Ralston's Route, April 26–May 1, 2003

START: Ralston parks his truck on April 25. The following morning, he rides his bike 15 miles to Blue John Canyon.

Trailhead to Horseshoe Canyon

Ralston is taken in a helicopter for medical care.

Ralston encounters a group of hikers.

HORSESHOE CANYON

Ralston rappels down this 65-foot cliff one-handed.

Big Drop

STUCK: Ralston is stuck here from April 26 to May 1.

BLUE JOHN CANYON

Trailhead to Blue John Canyon

Ralston parks his bike and starts hiking through the canyon.

North

| 0 | | 2 miles |
| 0 | | 2 kilometers |

KEY

— Ralston's bike ride

- - - Ralston's hike into the canyon

····· Ralston's escape

This photograph of Aron Ralston was taken in Aspen, Colorado, in 2005. He can attach several different hand units, including ones specially designed for climbing, to his prosthetic arm.

Aron Ralston

Born:

October 27, 1975, in Indiana

Turning point:

Moved to Colorado at age 12 and fell in love with the outdoors

Education:

Studied mechanical engineering, French, and classical piano at Carnegie Mellon University

True grit:

Two years after his accident, Ralston completed his quest to solo-climb all 59 of Colorado's 14,000-foot-tall mountains.

Favorite books:

Desert Solitaire: A Season in the Wilderness, Edward Abbey

Into the Wild, Jon Krakauer

Touching the Void: The True Story of One Man's Miraculous Survival, Joe Simpson

Kiss or Kill: Confessions of a Serial Climber, Mark F. Twight

Author of:

Between a Rock and a Hard Place

They say about his book:

"Ralston writes very well. His thoughts ricochet from anger to anguish to acceptance. He recounts the joy of risk, and he takes full responsibility," says Grace Lichtenstein of the *Washington Post*.

Joe Simpson and Simon Yates's Route on Siula Grande, June 1985

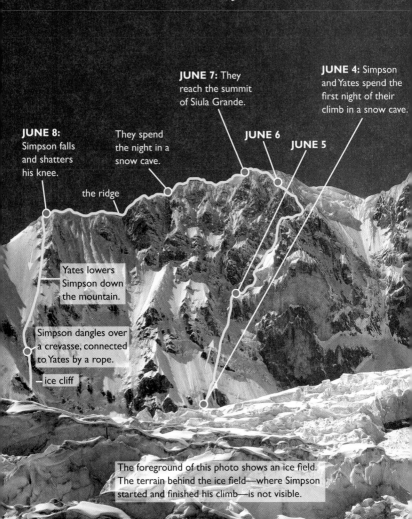

JUNE 4: Simpson and Yates spend the first night of their climb in a snow cave.

JUNE 7: They reach the summit of Siula Grande.

JUNE 6

JUNE 5

JUNE 8: Simpson falls and shatters his knee.

They spend the night in a snow cave.

the ridge

Yates lowers Simpson down the mountain.

Simpson dangles over a crevasse, connected to Yates by a rope.

— ice cliff

The foreground of this photo shows an ice field. The terrain behind the ice field—where Simpson started and finished his climb—is not visible.

BEYOND THE BRINK

In 1985, Joe Simpson and Simon Yates traveled
to Peru to climb an icy peak in the Andes.
When disaster struck at 20,000 feet, it put their
partnership to the ultimate test—and forced
Simpson into an epic battle for survival.

6

On Top of the World

Step after heavy step, the steel-toothed crampons on Joe Simpson's boots bit into the snow. His lungs pulled at the thin air, gathering energy for the final yards of the climb. At last he joined his partner, Simon Yates, at the top of Siula Grande, one of the tallest peaks in the Andes mountains.

The two climbers were exhausted but thrilled. They had come to Peru to make the first-ever ascent of Siula Grande's dangerous west face. For four days they had fought through snowstorms, scaled walls

Joe Simpson (left) and Simon Yates pose in Peru in 2003. Eighteen years earlier, they had climbed the west face of Siula Grande, a mountain in the Andes chain in Peru.

of ice, and dodged falling rocks. Now, on June 7, 1985, they stood at the summit.

Simpson and Yates allowed themselves a minute to soak up the sun. Then they turned to the task ahead. They had to get down safely, and both climbers knew that the descent is often more dangerous than the climb itself.

At 24, Simpson understood the dangers of mountain climbing. While growing up in Great Britain, he had read accounts of failed expeditions. Ropes pulled loose from the rock face and sent experienced mountaineers tumbling to their deaths. Avalanches buried people or swept them off mountainsides. Unexpected blizzards trapped climbers until they froze to death.

Simpson found the stories terrifying—and fascinating. He remembered thinking,

"God, this is so awful . . . there must be something really good in this if they think this is worth enduring."

As a young man, Simpson discovered for himself the thrill of climbing. He practiced until he felt comfortable on almost any mountainside. He scaled dozens of peaks in Britain and in the Alps of central Europe.

In the early 1980s he met Yates, who shared his passion. By 1985, they felt they were ready for Siula Grande.

After reaching the summit that day in June, the climbers cut their celebration short. Yates nodded toward a wall of dark clouds approaching from the east. They needed to get moving before the blizzard hit.

Simpson and Yates climbed Siula Grande, which rises 20,813 feet above sea level. At that altitude, the air contains less than half as much oxygen as it does at sea level. Breathing the thin air can cause confusion and fatigue. Severe altitude sickness can kill a climber.

Simpson and Yates wanted to descend by an easier route than the one they had climbed. They planned to follow the ridge north until they found a more gradual slope down the west side of the mountain. If all went well, in two days they would be sleeping in a warm tent in the valley below.

They started moving cautiously along the ridge. On either side, the mountain dropped away steeply. One slip and a climber could slide thousands of feet to certain death.

To guard against a fall, Simpson and Yates linked themselves with a 150-foot rope. The rope was tied to their climbing harnesses. The harnesses were strapped around their waists and thighs. If one of them slipped, the other would try to throw himself off the opposite side of the ridge to stop his partner's fall.

Two women climb a mountain in Peru. Like Simpson and Yates, these climbers have linked themselves with a rope tied to their climbing harnesses.

A climber carves a cave in the snow. On expeditions like the Siula Grande ascent, climbers often sleep in snow caves. That way, they don't have to carry tents.

Within an hour, a blinding storm engulfed the ridge. Progress slowed to a crawl. The frightened climbers decided to camp for the night. They carved out a small cave in a drift of snow and slipped into their sleeping bags.

By morning, they had eaten the last of their food. The fuel they used to melt snow into drinking water was gone. There would be nothing to eat or drink until they escaped the mountain.

A climber in Chile uses ice axes to ascend an ice wall. The crampons attached to his boots have spikes that carve into the ice, giving him a foothold on a nearly vertical cliff.

7
Over the Edge

Simpson took the lead the next morning, pushing his way through deep snow. The storm had let up during the night. But the men still had to move slowly on the narrow ridge. Several times the soft snow gave way, and Simpson slid spread-eagled down one side of the ridge. Each time, he dug in with ice axes and crampons and came to a rest before the rope tightened. Then he clawed his way back up to the ridge.

In mid-morning, Simpson hit another delay. The ridge in front of him dropped off suddenly into an icy cliff. He peered over the edge at a 25-foot drop. At the bottom of the cliff, the ridge continued in a gentle slope. But getting to the bottom was not going to be easy.

The cliff looked treacherous to Simpson. He wanted to pound a stake into the top and lower himself down by rope. But he decided that the snow was too loose to hold the stake. He would have to climb down with only his ice axes and his crampons.

Simpson decided not to wait for Yates, who was at least 100 feet behind. He knelt on the edge of the cliff with his back to the drop-off. He hammered his axes into the snow until they held. Gripping the ax handles

Yates and Simpson's progress along the ridge of Siula
Grande was blocked by a steep ice cliff like the one
shown above.

for support, he lowered his legs slowly over the cliff. He kicked the toe spikes of his crampons into the ice-encrusted wall of the cliff and shifted his weight onto the spikes. They held. One by one he found a new place for his ice axes right at the edge of the cliff. Then he leaned over and swung the ax in his left hand into the ice wall. The blade refused to bite, so he swung again.

As he tried to jam the blade into the ice, the ax in his right hand suddenly broke loose. The jolt twisted his crampons out of the frozen wall. He dropped feet first through the air and slammed into the ridge below.

Simpson screamed as an explosion of pain tore through his right leg. He slid to a stop on the east face of the ridge. He touched his knee through his wind pants and felt like he was going to throw up. The impact had rammed a bone in his lower leg—his tibia—up through the knee joint. His ankle was also broken.

Minutes later, Yates appeared at the top of the cliff. "What happened? Are you okay?" he asked.

"No," Simpson replied. "I've broken my leg."

Yates stared at Simpson for what seemed a very long time.

Simpson tried to stay as calm as possible, but he was panicked and fighting hysteria. He knew he was in deep trouble, perhaps just hours from death. There was no way that Yates would be able to get him off the mountain. Ordinarily, it would require a team of eight to ten men to rescue a climber with the kind of injuries he had.

Simpson and Yates had no way to call for help, so a rescue team wasn't an option. Although Yates could probably get down the mountain by himself, Simpson would freeze to death before his partner could return with help.

Simpson knew that Yates couldn't stay with him, either. If he did, both climbers were likely to die.

Yates climbed carefully down the ice cliff and stood beside Simpson. The two friends said almost nothing to each other. Simpson desperately wanted to know what Yates planned to do. But he was afraid to ask.

Eventually, Yates began to make his way along the east face toward a lower point on the ridge ahead. As he walked sideways along the slope, he made an extra effort to stomp a trail in the snow. Simpson followed as best he could, using his ice axes as canes. Again and again he stuck both ice axes in the snowy ridge and then took an awkward hop sideways. His shattered knee throbbed and progress was grindingly slow. But through the pain came a glimmer of hope: Yates was not going to desert him.

Pictured above is a ridgeline in the Peruvian Andes, much like the one where Simpson shattered his knee. A ridge is a long, narrow strip connecting two slopes of a mountain.

8
Cut Loose

Simpson and Yates struggled along the side of the mountain for hours, making their way slowly back to the ridge. Finally, the men found the route they had been looking for. The mountain dropped from the ridge into a smooth slope. The slope descended 3,000 feet to an ice field that led back to their base camp.

If they made it down the slope, survival was a real possibility.

Shivering in the cold, the climbers studied the route. It was too steep for Simpson to manage with his broken leg. Yates would have to lower him by rope. To hold his partner's weight, he would need a way to brace himself.

With another storm approaching, the climbers got to work. They carved a bucket-shaped seat in the snow to support Yates. Simpson tied two 150-foot ropes together. Yates fed the line through a belay plate attached to his harness. Shaped like a big belt buckle, the belay plate would allow him to control the speed of the rope as he lowered Simpson.

Simpson attached an end of the rope to his harness. He lay down on his chest on the slope with Yates dug into the seat above

A man uses a rope and a belay plate to protect his climbing partner. The belay plate can lock the rope to stop a climber from falling. After Simpson's accident, Yates reversed the usual technique. He sat above Simpson and used a rope and a belay plate to lower him down the mountain.

him. Yates let out some rope. Simpson began to slide feet first down the slope. He moved slowly at first. Yates gradually increased the speed.

After 300 feet, Simpson kicked his good leg into the snow to take the weight off the rope. Yates climbed carefully down to meet him. After digging a new seat in the snow they repeated the entire process.

The lowering was agony for Simpson. His right boot often caught in the snow, wrenching his broken leg. When the pain was more than he could bear, he screamed into the gathering storm.

The daylight began to fade. The wind picked up and snow started falling again. Yates lowered Simpson still faster, trying to beat the weather.

After many repetitions, they figured they were nearing the ice field. But the storm made it impossible to see what lay below.

Again, Simpson began his painful slide down the mountainside. This time he felt the slope grow steeper. Yates was taking more and more of his weight. Simpson's instincts told him he was headed for a cliff. He screamed a warning, but Yates could not hear him. He dug his axes into the snow, desperately trying to slow his slide. They failed to bite in the loose powder.

Suddenly, Simpson felt the mountainside drop away beneath him. He jerked to a halt, twisting in his harness 15 feet below the edge of a cliff.

When he recovered from the jolt, Simpson made a desperate attempt to climb back up the rope. His frozen hands were useless.

He tried to reach the wall of the ice cliff just six feet away. He didn't come close.

Dangling helplessly on the rope, Simpson felt all hope slip away. Fifty feet below his feet loomed the opening to a crevasse, a gaping crack in the ice.

High above Simpson, Yates struggled with his own dilemma. He could tell from the taut rope that Simpson had dropped off a cliff. But he couldn't climb down to help. If he left his seat, Simpson's weight would jerk him down the slope. There was no way he could haul his partner back up. Yates's strength was fading, and he could barely feel his hands. Several of his fingers were turning black with frostbite.

For more than an hour, Yates held on, hoping that Simpson could somehow take

Two climbers confront an ice cliff in the Andes. In the
unpredictable landscape of a frozen mountainside,
smooth slopes can suddenly give way to treacherous cliffs.

his weight off the line. But the seat was breaking apart in the snow. Yates struggled frantically to keep his footing. Soon, he knew, he would slip. Then gravity would do its deadly work.

Finally, Yates made the only choice he had left. With the snow giving way beneath him, he dug frantically in his backpack.

He found a knife and cut the rope.

A climber approaches a crevasse in the Andes. After
Simpson fell off a slope on Siula Grande, he dangled
over a deep crevasse. Crevasses form when an icy
glacier splits apart as it moves down a mountain.

In this scene from the 2003 documentary *Touching the Void,* an actor playing Joe Simpson screams in pain as he is lowered down the mountain.

9
Into the Depths

Simpson fell with his face to the sky. The rope tumbled after him. *So this is it!* he thought. Then he slammed to a stop, landing hard on his backpack.

Lights flashed in his head as snow and ice tumbled down on him. The impact had punched the air from his lungs. Finally, he was able to gulp a breath.

He lay still, stunned. He had slammed onto a ledge of ice inside the crevasse. Looking up, he could see that he was about 50 feet deep inside the icy cavern. He had fallen more than 100 feet—and survived!

He carefully felt around the ledge, afraid he might slip off. He quickly took stock of his gear. He was out of food and water. But he still had his backpack with his sleeping bag inside. His ice axes hung from cords attached to his harness.

Simpson found an ice screw. Ice screws are thick metal screws designed to fit securely in ice. They can hold a person's weight. Simpson banged the ice screw into the wall of ice beside him. With his frozen fingers, he clumsily tied a safety line to it.

He turned on his headlamp and looked down. The beam disappeared into what seemed like a bottomless cave.

A climber explores a crevasse in the French Alps.
After Yates cut the rope connecting him to Simpson,
Simpson plunged 100 feet into a crevasse.

Then he remembered the rope tied at his waist. The other end was stuck high above him at the top of the crevasse. He began pulling it down. Finally, its other end dropped into his lap. He shined his headlamp on the end. The clean edge told him that Yates had cut it.

He was trapped. He turned his headlamp off and sat in the darkness.

As dawn filtered in the next morning, Simpson accepted the harsh truth. No help was coming. It was obvious that Yates thought he was dead. He considered his options. He could not climb up the ice wall with just one good leg. If he did nothing, it would likely take three days to freeze to death in this icy tomb.

That left one choice: he had to go down. He tied the rope onto the ice screw and fed the line through the belay plate on his harness. He tossed the line into the darkness below. If the rope reached the bottom, he might find another way out. If it didn't, he would slip off the end of it and fall to his death.

He took a deep breath and slid down the rope into the dim crevasse.

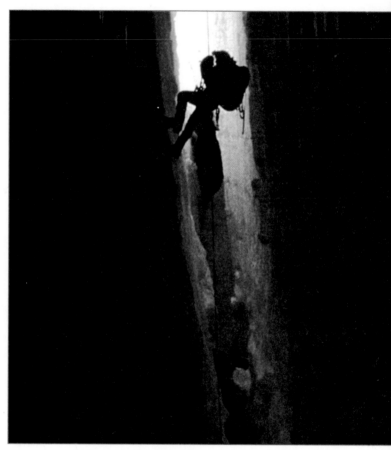

In this scene from *Touching the Void,* the actor playing Simpson lowers himself into the crevasse. As Simpson descended, he had no idea whether he had enough rope to reach the bottom.

10
The Long Crawl

Daylight faded the deeper Simpson dropped—50 feet, 60 feet, 70 feet. Finally, he worked up the courage to look down.

Just 15 feet below lay the bottom! In the distance he saw a steep cone of snow and ice rising from the crevasse floor. It rose 130 feet toward the sunlight. He let out a whoop that echoed in the cavern.

Simpson lowered himself the rest of the way. He dragged himself across the floor of ice and snow. Then he began to climb the cone, following the same pattern again and again. Bury the ice axes in the snow. Dig a foothold and hop up to it. Bury the ice axes a little higher. Dig another foothold and hop again.

Five hours later, Simpson's climbing helmet rose above the edge of the crevasse into the sunlight. He gazed around at the stunning beauty of the mountains. He climbed onto level ground, rolled onto his back, and rested.

But relief was short-lived. To get to base camp he still had to cross a glacier laced with crevasses. Beyond that lay miles of moraine—long, wide fields of boulders and rocks.

Every challenge he overcame seemed to be followed by another. And he was quickly losing his strength. It had been two days since he had tasted food or water.

Simpson decided he would probably die on the glacier. But the thought no longer filled him with fear. A voice spoke up in his mind, forceful and confident. It insisted that he needed to move and told him exactly how to do it. He sat down and pulled himself across the snow in a crab-like crawl that kept his crampons from catching and twisting his broken leg.

Simpson turned his ordeal into a contest. He picked a landmark—a rock or crevasse. He guessed how much time it would take to reach it. Then he raced the clock to reach his goal. Yard by yard he dragged himself in the direction of help. The voice urged him on.

Night fell on the lonely glacier. Simpson dug a small snow cave and climbed into his sleeping bag to rest.

Simpson appeared in several scenes in *Touching the Void*. Here, he lies on a moraine, a loose pile of rocks and gravel left behind by a glacier.

11
Race Against Death

The next morning, Simpson resumed his grueling journey. After hours more of crab-walking, he reached the moraine. It was the last major obstacle between Simpson and the base camp. He saw right away that he couldn't crawl across the uneven, rocky terrain. He would have to hop on his good leg. He strapped his sleeping pad around his injured leg to brace it.

Simpson hopped as best he could. He leaned over to use his ice axes as canes. Still, he stumbled and fell time after time.

He slammed into the rocks and screamed in pain. He made slow, bruising progress.

Night fell. He flopped among the rocks, confused and helpless. He gave up for the night and crawled into his sleeping bag.

The next morning, Simpson had an alarming thought: What if Yates had already left? A companion, Richard Hawking, had been guarding the tents while Simpson and Yates climbed Siula Grande. Wouldn't they just pack up and leave as soon as Yates had recovered from the climb?

Simpson's strength was running out. Pain, exhaustion, and thirst blended into relentless agony. The voice in his head commanded him to hurry. But his body struggled to obey. He fell and got up—again and again and again.

As the afternoon gave way to nightfall, Simpson began to hallucinate. He heard the voices of friends and family members. He forgot where he was or where he was going. He knew only that he had to keep moving. All he wanted was to make sure that he did not die alone.

It was about 1 A.M. when he got a whiff of an awful smell. He raised a glove to his face and sniffed. It was human waste. It took a moment for him to understand what that meant. He was lying in the spot they had used as a toilet—near base camp. He peered into the darkness. Were the tents still there?

"SIMON!" Simpson cried.

There was no answer.

"Help me!"

He noticed something glowing, but wondered whether it was just his imagination. Then he heard voices. He saw flashlights moving nearby. He tried to call out again but started sobbing.

"Joe! Is that you? JOE!" It was Yates's voice. His headlamp swept the darkness. Then he was beside Simpson, holding and comforting him. "It'll be okay," he said.

"I've got you, I have you, you're safe …"

Yates and Hawking carried Simpson to a tent. Yates shook his head in disbelief.

Simpson knew his partner felt terrible for leaving him on the mountain. Now he tried to comfort him. "Thanks, Simon," Simpson croaked. "I'd have done the same."

Doctors eventually performed six surgeries on Simpson's shattered leg. They told him he would be lucky to walk again. Two years later, he was climbing mountains once more.

In 1988, he published *Touching the Void*. The book is a gut-wrenching account of his ordeal. It was turned into a film in 2003.

Other climbers faulted Yates for what he had done, but not Simpson. He credited Yates with saving his life and dedicated his book "To Simon Yates for a debt I can never repay."

In this scene from *Touching the Void,* Simpson reenacts his climb out of the crevasse.

Joe Simpson

Born:

August 13, 1960, in Kuala Lumpur. His father was in the British army.

Grew up:

All over the place, including Ireland; Germany; and Sheffield, Great Britain

Inspiration:

Read a book about mountain climbing at age 14

Education:

Studied English literature at Edinburgh University

Favorite books:

His Dark Materials trilogy, Philip Pullman
The Killer Angels, Michael Shaara
Lonesome Dove, Larry McMurtry
The Old Man and the Sea, Ernest Hemingway
all of Bruce Chatwin's books

Author of:

The Beckoning Silence
Dark Shadows Falling
Touching the Void: The True Story of One Man's Miraculous Survival
This Game of Ghosts: The Sequel to Touching the Void
and other books

They say about his book:

"Simpson's dramatic tale of survival is now the stuff of legend," says Peter Stanford of the *Daily Telegraph*.

A Conversation with Author
Sean McCollum

Q *Had you heard about Aron Ralston or Joe Simpson or before you started working on this book?*

A Aron Ralston lives here in Boulder, Colorado, where I live. He's something of a local folk hero. And I read Joe Simpson's book *Touching the Void* when it first came out in 1988. Then I saw the film in 2003.

Q *How did you go about researching this book?*

A The men were not available for interviews, so I did a tremendous amount of research. Both of these guys wrote books about their experiences, but that was just my starting point. I had to keep digging. Fortunately, they have given many interviews and told the details of their stories many, many times. So I read and viewed everything I could find about them. I took careful notes, and then I started writing.

Q *What was the most surprising thing you learned?*

A The procedure for cutting off my own hand, if necessary. And that you should let the salts settle for a while before drinking your pee.

Q *Extreme adventures like mountain climbing are dangerous. So why do you think people go on them?*

A I think so-called "extreme adventurers" are drawn to the intensity and clarity they experience. For those hours or days when they are climbing, canyoneering, skiing, paragliding, or whatever, they don't worry about bad grades, grumpy bosses, overdue bills, or jealous sweethearts. They must focus on what they are doing right then and there. They must! If they lose their concentration, there is chance they'll be injured or dead.

Q *Do you hike, climb, or do any other outdoor sports?*

A Yes! I rock climb, backpack, ski, snowshoe, and have hiked up about 20 of Colorado's fourteeners—the mountains here that rise above 14,000 feet.

Q *Could you have done what Ralston or Simpson did?*

A Not a chance. There's a reason their stories grab people's attention. That kind of death-defying resilience is very, very rare.

Q *What do you think it was that made these guys so resilient?*

A Both Simpson and Ralston refused to get completely freaked out and paralyzed by their dilemmas. Instead, they focused on taking little steps and doing little things to keep their minds occupied. That is a powerful strategy that can help any of us remain resilient when we face a situation that seems overwhelming: break up the challenge into small steps and never surrender to despair.

Q *How do you think these guys were affected by their ordeals?*

A For Ralston, his experience seemed to force him to look hard at why he took such high-risk challenges. He's still climbing mountains and seeking outdoor adventure. But he's more thoughtful now about what he does and why he does it— especially since he's now married and a father.

Simpson also kept climbing, but he became more philosophical and less of a daredevil. He's also become a best-selling author. His books have chronicled the lives—and deaths—of many of the great mountain climbers of his generation.

Q *Do you think the men made some bad decisions that resulted in their ordeals?*

A Both Simpson and Ralston are the first to admit they made mistakes that put them in danger. Ralston acknowledges he should have left detailed information about where he was going. His trip was tame compared to his past adventures. But going solo to remote places always has risks.

Simpson's situation was more complex. One error Simpson and Yates made was not packing enough supplies, especially gas to melt snow for drinking water. That put them in a race against time to get down a very treacherous mountain. They felt rushed and took chances. That led to Simpson falling from the ice cliff and shattering his knee.

Q *Do you think Yates made the right decision when he let Simpson fall?*

A Simpson knew firsthand the conditions his partner faced. He understood what happened and why. And he understood why Yates had to cut the rope. To my mind, their opinions are the only ones that matter.

What to Read Next

Fiction

Death Mountain, Sherry Shahan. (208 pages) *Two girls are lost in the Sierra Nevada Mountains in extreme lightning storms.*

Hatchet, Gary Paulsen. (192 pages) *A 13-year-old boy is the only survivor of a plane crash in the Canadian wilderness.* Paulsen also wrote several sequels: **Brian's Return** (144 pages), **Brian's Winter** (133 pages), **The River** (144 pages), **Brian's Hunt** (112 pages).

I Survived the Shark Attacks of 1916, Lauren Tarshis. (112 pages) *A great white shark is terrorizing the waters near Chet Roscoe's hometown.* Tarshis also wrote other tales of survival: **I Survived the Sinking of the Titanic, 1912** (112 pages); **I Survived Hurricane Katrina, 2005** (112 pages)

My Side of the Mountain, Jean Craighead George. (192 pages) *Teenager Sam Gribley runs away and lives in a hollow tree in the Catskill Mountains, with a falcon and a weasel as his companions.*

Peak, Roland Smith. (256 pages) *Fourteen-year-old Peak Marcello joins his father's expedition to climb Mount Everest.*

Touching Spirit Bear, Ben Mikaelsen. (320 pages) *Given the choice of going to jail or living alone on a remote Alaskan island, 15-year-old Cole Matthews chooses the island.*

Nonfiction

The Basic Essentials of Rock Climbing, Michael A. Strassman. (72 pages) *This beginner's guide includes diagrams and descriptions of footholds, handholds, and knots.*

The Boy Who Conquered Everest: The Jordan Romero Story, Jordan Romero and Katherine Blanc. (72 pages) *This is the true-life story of a 13-year-old who became the youngest person ever to climb Mount Everest.*

Shipwreck at the Bottom of the Earth, Jennifer Armstrong. (144 pages) *The story of the expedition of Sir Ernest Shackleton, who was trying to lead 27 sailors across Antarctica.*

Willy Whitefeather's Outdoor Survival Handbook for Kids, Willy Whitefeather. (104 pages) *This guide covers survival in the mountains, deserts, woods, and swamps.*

Books

Between a Rock and a Hard Place, Aron Ralston. (354 pages) *Aron Ralston's own account of his ordeal was the basis of the 2010 film* 127 Hours.

Touching the Void, Joe Simpson. (218 pages) *Joe Simpson's story of his experiences on Siula Grande was made into a documentary of the same name.*

Films and Videos

Canyonlands (2010). *This DVD, produced by National Geographic, presents an amazing tour of this 300,000-acre park.*

Survivor: The Aron Ralston Story with Tom Brokaw (2006). *This NBC News documentary includes video footage Ralston took while he was trapped in the canyon.*

Websites

http://www.americansouthwest.net/index.shtml
This guide to the rock structures and national monuments of the American Southwest includes hundreds of photographs.

http://www.touchingthevoid.co.uk
Joe Simpson's website includes articles, personal information, news, and photos.

http://www.abc-of-mountaineering.com
This site has mountaineering tips for experts and beginners. It also has information about the world's highest peaks and the equipment you'd need to climb them.

Glossary

ascend (uh-SEND) *verb* to move upward

belay (buh-LAY) *verb* to protect a climbing partner with a safety rope. A belaying device locks the rope so the climber attached to the rope cannot fall past a certain distance.

carabiner (kar-uh-BEEN-ur) *noun* a metal clip used to attach ropes and other gear

chockstone (CHOK-stone) *noun* a rock that is wedged in a gap

climbing harness (KLY-ming HAR-niss) *noun* a piece of equipment that attaches to a climber's chest or waist and legs. It's used to fasten a rope to the climber.

crampons (KRAM-ponz) *noun* spiked metal attachments to climbing boots that grip ice or snow

crevasse (kruh-VASS) *noun* a deep crack in the ice of a glacier

dehydration (dee-hye-DRAY-shuhn) *noun* a dangerous lack of water in the body

face (FACE) *noun* one side of a mountain

frostbite (FRAWST-bite) *noun* damage to the skin and flesh caused by extreme cold

glacier (GLAY-shur) *noun* a huge sheet of ice that moves slowly over land

hypothermia (hye-puh-THUR-mee-uh) *noun* dangerously low body temperature

moraine (muh-RAYN) *noun* piles of dirt and rocks that were left by a glacier

prosthetic (pross-THET-ik) *adjective* artificial and substituting for a missing part of the body

pulley (PUL-ee) *noun* a wheel with a groove for a rope; it can be used to lift loads more easily

rappel (ruh-PEL) *verb* to descend a cliff or the side of a mountain using a rope

ridge (RIJ) *noun* a long narrow upper edge of a mountain

slot canyon (SLOT KAN-yuhn) *noun* a canyon that is much deeper than it is wide

summit (SUHM-it) *noun* the highest point of a mountain

tendon (TEN-duhn) *noun* a strong band of tissue that joins a muscle to a bone

tourniquet (TUR-nuh-ket) *noun* a bandage twisted tightly around a wound to slow the loss of blood

trailhead (TRAYL-hed) *noun* the place where a trail begins

Metric Conversions

feet to meters: 1 ft is about 0.3 m

miles to kilometers: 1 mi is about 1.6 km

pounds to kilograms: 1 lb is about 0.45 kg

ounces to grams: 1 oz is about 28 g

degrees Fahrenheit (F°) to degrees Celsius (C°)

formula: $$\frac{5 \times (F° - 32)}{9} = C°$$

Sources

ESCAPE FROM BLUE JOHN CANYON

"Against All Odds," Grace Lichtenstein. *Washington Post*, September 26, 2004. (including quote on page 53)

"Aron Ralston Sacrifices His Right Arm to Save His Life," Jessica Strelitz. *Carnegie Mell Magazine*, Fall 2003.

"The Art of Survival: It's All in the Mind," Luke Leitch, *Sunday Times*, July 16, 2009. (including quote on page 4)

Between a Rock and a Hard Place, Aron Ralston. New York: Atria Books, 2004. (including quotes on pages 23, 49)

"Boyle to Direct Film About Climber Who Cut Off Arm." CBC News, January 18, 201●

"Catching Up with Aron Ralston," Joshua Kupetz. *Disaboom.com.*

"Cheating Death in Bluejohn Canyon," Shane Burrows. *Climb-Utah.com.*

"Climber Still Seeks Larger Meaning in His Epic Escape," Michael Brick. *New York Times*, March 31, 2009.

"Climber Who Amputated Arm Had No Choice," Associated Press. *USA Today*, May 2, 2003.

"Climber Who Cut Off Hand Looks Back," Michael Benoist. *National Geographic*, August 30, 2004.

"Colorado Hiker Who Amputated Arm Describes Ordeal." Internet Broadcasting Systems, May 8, 2003.

"Desperate Days in Blue John Canyon," Tom Brokaw. *Dateline NBC*, July 1, 2005.

"Episode 65: Aron Ralston," Andrew Denton. *Enough Rope with Andrew Denton*, October 25, 2004.

"Hanger Patient Aron Ralston's Story of Survival to Be Featured in New Movie." *Hanger.com*, November 5, 2010.

"Hiker Who Cut Off Arm: My Future Son Saved Me," Michael Inbar. *Todayshow.com*, December 8, 2009.

"The Man Who Cut Off His Own Arm," David Jones. Solo Syndication Limited, 2004.

"My Summit Problem," Aron Ralston. *OutsideOnline.com*, April 2006.

"Then & Now: Aron Ralston." *CNN*, June 19, 2005.

"Trapped," Aron Ralston. *OutsideOnline.com*, September 2004.

"127 Hours: The Aron Ralston Story." *Hanger.com*, 2005.

BEYOND THE BRINK

The Beckoning Silence, Joe Simpson. Seattle: The Mountaineers Books, 2003.

"The Climb of His Life," Steve Meacham. *Sydney Morning Herald*, February 28, 2005.

Dark Shadows Falling, Joe Simpson. Seattle: The Mountaineers Books, 1997. (including quote on page 5)

"Episode 49: Joe Simpson," Andrew Denton. *Enough Rope with Andrew Denton*, July 5, 2004. (including quotes on page 71)

"How We Met: Joe Simpson and Simon Yates," Nerys Lloyd-Pierce. *The Independent on Sunday Magazine*, February 23, 1997.

"Joe Simpson: High Flyer," Rob Sharp. *The Independent*, October 6, 2007.

"Joe Simpson: My Journey Back into the Void," Joe Simpson. *Telegraph*, October 22, 2007.

"Joe Simpson: The Man Who Came Back from His Icy Grave," Charles Arthur. *The Independent*, December 6, 2003. (including quote on page 60)

"Joe Simpson: Siula Grande Survivor." *ABC of Mountaineering*.

"The Man Who Fell to Earth," Jasper Rees. *Telegraph*, November 12, 2003.

"Notable Mountain Climbing Accidents Analyzed by Experts," Robert Speik. *Traditional Mountaineering*, 2004–2006.

"Return to Siula Grande," Kevin Macdonald. *Guardian*, November 21, 2003.

Touching the Void, Joe Simpson. New York: Harper & Row, 1988. (including quotes on pages 98, 99)

Touching the Void, DVD, directed by Kevin MacDonald. IFC Films, 2004. (including quote on page 97)

Index